Mrs. Inly
2002

Karen's Hurricane

**Other books by
Ann M. Martin**

P. S. Longer Letter Later
(written with Paula Danziger)
Leo the Magnificat
Rachel Parker, Kindergarten Show-off
Eleven Kids, One Summer
Ma and Pa Dracula
Yours Turly, Shirley
Ten Kids, No Pets
With You and Without You
Me and Katie (the Pest)
Stage Fright
Inside Out
Bummer Summer

For older readers:

Missing Since Monday
Just a Summer Romance
Slam Book

Little Sister

Karen's Hurricane
Ann M. Martin

Illustrations by Susan Crocca Tang

A
LITTLE APPLE
PAPERBACK

SCHOLASTIC INC.
New York Toronto London Auckland Sydney
Mexico City New Delhi Hong Kong

The author gratefully acknowledges
Gabrielle Charbonnet
for her help
with this book.

ISBN 0-590-52379-1

12 11 10 9 8 7 6 5 4 3 2 1   9/9 0 1 2 3 4/0

Printed in the U.S.A.   40
First Scholastic printing, September 1999

Thunder and Lightning

"Ladies and gentlemen!" said a booming voice. "The world's greatest girl daredevil, the Amazing Karen, will now perform her most death-defying stunt."

I was wearing a gigundoly beautiful purple sequined leotard. I climbed up a tall ladder and into the end of a big cannon. I waved to the cheering crowd.

"The Amazing Karen will now be shot out of the cannon, all the way over a twelve-story building," said the voice. "And she will not be scared at all!"

The crowd cheered even louder. I was so, so brave. Waving one last time, I slid down into the cannon. I could hear someone lighting a fuse. And then —

Boom!

My eyes popped open. I was not wearing a sequined leotard. I was wearing pajamas. I was not in a cannon. I was in bed. I was not the Amazing Karen. I was plain old Karen Brewer. My wonderful moment waving to the crowd, my beautiful leotard, the cannon — all of it had been a dream.

Suddenly lightning flashed outside my window, lighting up my room. An instant later —

Boom!

One thing had not been a dream — the great big *boom* at the end.

And I realized that I was not so, so brave. I was scared.

Just then the door to my room flew open and my little brother rushed in.

"Karen, Karen!" said Andrew. "Save me!" He leaped onto my bed and scrambled underneath the covers. He pulled the sheet over his head.

Now, if there is one thing in the whole wide world that will make a big sister feel brave, it is her little brother feeling more scared than she is.

I knew I had to be there for Andrew.

"It is okay," I said calmly, patting his back. "It is just a little storm."

Lightning flashed. *Boom!*

Under the sheet, Andrew whimpered.

"Okay, it is kind of a big storm," I said. "But we are perfectly safe. Thunder is just a loud noise. It cannot hurt you." (That is what Mommy used to tell me, back when I was little. I am seven now. Andrew is only four going on five.)

"What about the lightning?" asked Andrew's voice.

"Lightning can be dangerous if you are outside," I said. "But we are inside, safe and cozy and warm."

Andrew poked his head out from under the sheet.

Flash! *Boom!* went the storm.

"How about this?" I said. "Listen. We will figure out how far away the lightning is from us. When you see a flash of lightning, start counting slowly."

Flash!

"One Mississippi, two Mississippi, three Mississippi, four Mississippi, five Mississippi," Andrew and I counted together. Then, *boom!*

"We counted to five," I said. "That means the storm is about five miles away from us."

"Really?" said Andrew. "Gosh, that is pretty far."

I could tell he felt better, knowing the lightning was so far away.

There was another flash, and we counted again. This time we reached eight.

"The storm is moving away from us," I said.

Andrew nodded.

"Do you think you can go back to your own bedroom and sleep now?" I asked.

Andrew nodded again. He crawled out

from under my sheet and slid out of bed. He padded toward the door. Then he turned around.

"Thanks, Karen," he said. "You are a good big sister."

"You are welcome, Andrew," I said. "You are a good little brother."

Andrew left the room. I was asleep again so quickly, I do not even remember my head hitting the pillow.

Underneath the Oak

"Hi, Hannie!" I called. It was the next morning, before school. Nancy Dawes and I ran to meet our other best friend, Hannie Papadakis. (I will tell you more about them — and me — soon.) She was standing beneath the big old oak tree in the corner of the schoolyard.

Hannie was holding something up to her mouth. She took a big breath and — *tweet!*

"Wow!" I said as we reached her. "Some whistle! How did you do that?"

"With an acorn cap," Hannie said. She

showed Nancy and me how to put our thumbs together to make a little *V* shape. Then we each put an acorn cap behind our *V*s and blew hard into them.

Tweet!

"Wow!" I said again. "Loud."

Hannie nodded. "Yup. My daddy showed me how to do that."

I looked around us. Scattered all over the ground were acorns. So were sticks and branches. One of the branches was pretty big. It was much longer than I am.

"The storm last night hurt our tree," I said, frowning.

I called it our tree, because the Three Musketeers — Hannie, Nancy, and I — played under it a lot. It was a huge, beautiful old oak, with a trunk that was so big that the three of us could not reach all the way around it while holding hands. I know because we had tried.

Way high up, the trunk split into three main branches — one for each of us. The oak gave us shade in the summer, and it protected us from drizzle in the spring. In the fall its leaves turned bright red and yellow, and in the winter its branches looked black and spooky against the white snow.

Hannie, Nancy, and I have played hide-and-seek behind the old oak and told one another our most secret secrets underneath it. I have even cried beneath its branches, and somehow crying under the old oak always made me feel better. All year round it was just about the best tree in the whole world. It was our friend.

I looked up into its branches. Even though it was only September, many of them were bare. I had not noticed it before, but our tree was beginning to look kind of scraggly.

"Hey, you guys," I said, peering up. "Have you noticed — "

At that moment the bell rang, and Hannie and Nancy ran to line up. I ran after them. Later I would have a chance to tell them I was afraid our tree was not healthy.

"Class, I have an announcement to make," said Ms. Colman. Ms. Colman is my second-grade teacher. She is the best teacher in the world. She is always kind. That is a very good thing in a teacher.

"Oh, goody!" I said (not too loudly). I wiggled in my seat. I love Ms. Colman's announcements.

"This Friday will be Stoneybrook Academy's first annual Fix-Up Day," said Ms. Colman. "We will not have class that day. Instead, we will join the rest of the school in sprucing up the buildings and grounds."

Hands shot up around the classroom.

"Are we going to help fix a building or some ground?" asked Ian Johnson.

"If we are fixing up the ground, I call dibs on the bulldozer," said Bobby Giannelli.

The other boys started arguing about who would get to drive the bulldozer.

"If the boys fix the ground," said Sara Ford, "then we girls will fix the building. Will we be allowed on the roof, Ms. Colman? I lost a tennis ball up there once. It is probably still there."

"Will we have to wash the windows?" asked Jannie Gilbert.

"I do not do windows," said Pamela Harding.

Ms. Colman laughed. "You will not have to wash any windows, Pamela. And I am sorry, Bobby, but no one will be driving a bulldozer."

Ms. Colman went on to explain that each class in the school would work on a special project to help make our school look fresh and pretty.

Already my feet were tapping. I was getting excited. I am an excellent fixer-upper. I often help my big-house Nannie and my little-house nanny with cleaning and organizing. Plus I am good at decorating and painting and making things look beautiful. This project was perfect for me.

Oops! I just realized. I have not told you about my two houses yet (or about my nanny and my Nannie). Before I go any further, I will have to do that.

My Two Families

A long, long time ago, when I was little, my mommy, my daddy, Andrew, and I lived together in a big house here in Stoneybrook, Connecticut. Then Mommy and Daddy decided they could not live together anymore. So they got a divorce. It was a sad time for Andrew and me. Mommy, Andrew, and I moved out of the big house to a little house (also in Stoneybrook). Daddy stayed at the big house. (It is where he grew up.)

After awhile Mommy met a nice man named Seth Engle, and they got married.

That made him my stepfather, and he came to live with us in the little house. He brought along his cat, Rocky, and his dog, Midgie.

Then Daddy married a woman named Elizabeth Thomas. She became my stepmother. And guess what? Elizabeth already had not one, not two, not three, but *four* kids. They are Sam and Charlie, who are in high school; Kristy, who is in middle school; and David Michael, who is in second grade like me, but at a different school.

Then Daddy and Elizabeth adopted Emily Michelle from the faraway country of Vietnam. She is two and a half. So she is my little sister.

There were so many people at the big house that Nannie, Elizabeth's mother, came to help take care of everyone. Nannie also helps with the pets: David Michael's gigundo puppy, Shannon; Pumpkin, our new kitten; some fish; Bob, Andrew's hermit crab; and my rat, Emily Junior. (I love my pet rat.)

Andrew and I spend every other month with Mommy and Seth in the little house. We live with Daddy at the big house during the other months.

Because Andrew and I move back and forth, we have two of a lot of things. We have two houses and two families, two mommies, two daddies, two cats, and two dogs. We have a Nannie (my stepgrandmother) at the big house, and a nanny (named Merry Perkins) at the little house. I have two stuffed cats, Moosie and Goosie. I have two best friends, Hannie and Nancy. (Hannie lives across the street and one house down from the big house. Nancy lives next door to the little house.) I even have two pairs of glasses — blue ones for reading, and pink ones for the rest of the time. After Ms. Colman read a book called *Jacob Two-Two Meets the Hooded Fang* to our class, I made up special nicknames for my brother and me. I call us Andrew Two-Two and Karen Two-Two. I bet you can guess why.

Now Ms. Colman was telling our class how the Stoneybrook Academy students would help on Fix-Up Day.

"Older grades will paint hallways and lockers," Ms. Colman said. "The sixth grade will design and paint a mural in the cafeteria."

My class ooohed. I hoped we would get to do something like paint a mural.

"The younger grades, including the second grade, will work in the yard, making the outside of our school as beautiful as the inside," Ms. Colman went on. "Mr. Berger's second-grade class will collect litter, rake the paths, and spread new bark chips in the swings area. Our class will plant some new shrubs. Together we will make the school grounds look terrific."

"Yea!" Everyone cheered. Planting shrubs was definitely better than picking up trash. I hoped our new shrubs would have flowers on them. Or maybe they would be berry bushes.

My hand shot up. "Ms. Colman, can

we plant raspberry bushes, or blueberry bushes, or strawberry bushes, or blackberry bushes?" I said.

Ms. Colman smiled. "That is a fun idea, Karen," she said. "But I think the fix-up committee has chosen other plants that will not require much upkeep."

"Drat," I said.

"Besides, strawberries grow on vines, not on bushes," Ms. Colman added kindly.

"Can we plant strawberry vines to grow up our fences?" I asked hopefully.

My teacher smiled and shook her head. "I am afraid not."

"Drat," I said again.

You know, planting shrubs was better than raking paths, but it was not as good as painting a mural. We did not even get to choose the bushes or shrubs ourselves. I wished my class could do something *really* special for our school. I would have to think about this.

Hurricane Karen

When I got home that afternoon, I found Merry, my nanny, alone in the kitchen. (Mommy has a new job at the crafts center in town. My stepfather, Seth, works all day as a carpenter and furniture-maker. So Merry takes care of Andrew and me until Mommy and Seth get home. I love Merry.)

"Where is Andrew?" I asked. I do not miss Andrew except when I am expecting to see him. Then I do.

"He is at Ezra's house," said Merry. "Are

you hungry, Karen? Would you like a snack?"

"Yes, please," I said. I am always hungry after school.

Merry served me a snack of cream cheese on celery sticks, and a glass of juice. I dug in. I ate my snack, pretending that I was a rabbit eating in someone's garden. I tried to wiggle my ears a little.

"Karen, when you are done with your celery, could you help me make a salad for dinner tonight?" Merry asked.

"Sure," I said, crunching away.

After I finished, I stood on the stepstool by the sink. Merry handed me a head of lettuce. "Tear up the leaves into bite-size pieces and drop them in the salad spinner for washing. I will cut the tomatoes."

After a minute, Merry said, "I like to have music on when I work in the kitchen. Is that okay with you?"

I nodded.

Merry switched on the radio on the windowsill. Violins were playing a soft tune.

"Some like it hot, but I prefer classical," said Merry, smiling. "That is a line from an old movie."

"Oh," I said. Merry is just full of interesting tidbits like that. "I will say that myself sometime."

The music ended, and an announcer's voice came on the radio. "On the weather front, the North Carolina coast braces for what is shaping up to be the worst storm of the year."

I ripped a lettuce leaf and threw it in the spinner.

"The National Weather Center has issued a hurricane watch for the entire coast of North and South Carolina," the radio announcer said. "There is a sixty-percent chance that the hurricane will make landfall on the Carolina coast within the next seventy-two hours."

Gosh, I said to myself. A hurricane. That must be exciting for those people down in the Carolinas. I ripped a leaf and tossed it in

20

the spinner. I ripped another leaf and got ready to toss.

"The governor of North Carolina has urged residents of coastal areas to prepare for possible evacuation procedures, as the state readies for the onset of Hurricane Karen."

My lettuce leaf flew out of my hand and onto the floor, missing the spinner completely. "Hurricane Karen!" I exclaimed. "Oh my gosh!"

What Happens in a Hurricane?

"Hannie!" Nancy and I ran across the school playground to our friend. "Have you heard? I have a hurricane named after me!"

It was the next morning. Earlier, I had heard on the radio that Hurricane Karen had turned north. It might hit Virginia instead of North or South Carolina.

Hannie and Nancy had heard of Hurricane Karen too. (They had not tuned in to the morning news for updates, though.) They were almost as excited about Hurricane Karen as I was.

"Whooooosh!" I pretended to be a big wind. "Look out, everyone! Hurricane Karen is coming through!" I ran around the playground, whooshing and thundering. Hannie and Nancy laughed.

And now I bet you will never guess who else was excited about Hurricane Karen. Give up? It was Ms. Colman. When the bell rang, Hannie and Nancy and I raced into our classroom, as always.

"Guess what!" I shouted as I flung my books down on my desk. "I am a hurricane!"

"I thought of you when I heard about the hurricane," Ms. Colman said. "I think that after Ricky takes attendance, we can spend some time talking about hurricanes."

Ricky Torres is my pretend husband. We got married in the schoolyard a long time ago. We also sit next to each other in the front row of Ms. Colman's class — but not because we are married. It is because we are glasses-wearers. Natalie Springer is the other glasses-wearer, and she sits on the other side of Ricky.

Ricky stood up proudly and marched to Ms. Colman's desk to get the attendance book. When he had finished, Ms. Colman pulled down the large map of the United States that hangs in front of our blackboard.

"Here we are, in Connecticut," she said, pointing. "Here is North Carolina, and here is Virginia. It is not often that hurricanes come as far north as Virginia. Usually they strike states that are farther south, such as Florida, Georgia, or the Carolinas, or else they go into the Gulf of Mexico."

"Will Hurricane Karen hit Stoneybrook?" asked Jannie Gilbert in a scared voice.

"I am already here!" I piped up. Then I said loudly, "Whoooosh!"

"Indoor voice, Karen," said Ms. Colman. "It is not likely that Hurricane Karen will make it as far north as Connecticut, according to the weather experts. Hurricanes are very unpredictable, though. So it is difficult to say for certain where a hurricane will go."

Ms. Colman went on to explain a lot of interesting facts about hurricanes. (Ms. Colman is an excellent explainer.) First she told us what a hurricane is. It is a large, circular storm that spins around. Hurricanes always start forming over large bodies of water. She explained the difference between a hurricane and a tornado. (Tornadoes spin around too, but they are much, much smaller than hurricanes.) She showed us some pictures of hurricanes taken from space. They looked like giant pinwheels. A single hurricane can be much larger than the whole state of Connecticut.

On the edge of a hurricane it might be a little breezy and drizzly. But farther into the hurricane, it gets windier and rainier. There is thunder and lightning too. Then more wind and more rain, till it is blowing and coming down like crazy. At the very center of the hurricane, is the eye. In the eye, everything is calm. No wind, no rain.

But the hurricane is only half over. The

next thing you know, the eye has passed, and the other side of the hurricane moves in, with wind and rain and thunder and lightning just as fierce as before. Slowly, slowly the hurricane passes over, and the wind and rain die down, till finally it is only breezy and drizzly again.

Ms. Colman put another map over the large U.S. map. It was of the Atlantic Ocean and eastern United States. She said it was a hurricane tracking map. She drew a big red dot in the ocean near North Carolina, to show where Hurricane Karen had been yesterday. She drew another dot in the ocean near Virginia, to show where Hurricane Karen was now. Then she drew a red line between the two dots, to show the path of the hurricane. At lunchtime, she would listen to the radio in the teachers' room and find out where the hurricane was then. We would follow Hurricane Karen's progress, she explained, and track it on the map.

Finally Ms. Colman put the Saffir Simp-

son Hurricane Scale on the blackboard. The scale is for measuring hurricanes. Depending on how fast the wind is blowing, a hurricane is rated on a scale of one to five:

Category 1: winds 74–95 miles per hour
Category 2: winds 96–110 miles per hour
Category 3: winds 111–130 miles per hour
Category 4: winds 131–155 miles per hour
Category 5: winds 156+ miles per hour

I read the Saffir Simpson scale carefully. Ms. Colman said that Hurricane Karen was a Category 3 hurricane. That meant that it had winds from 111 to 130 miles per hour. Wow! When Mommy drives on the highway, she goes only 55 miles per hour. That meant that Hurricane Karen's winds were more than twice as fast as a car on a highway! Winds that strong and fierce would do a lot more damage than the storm we had heard the night before, and that was not even a tiny hurricane.

I could not imagine air moving that fast.

And I decided that I did *not* want to meet the real Hurricane Karen.

Fix-Up Day

On Friday morning Mommy and I watched the weather report on TV. (Usually we do not watch TV in the mornings, but Mommy made an exception because of my hurricane.)

The weatherwoman showed a picture of a big circular storm. It was still over the ocean.

"Hurricane Karen took a surprising turn last night," the woman said. "Only hours away from making landfall, the storm veered north, away from the Virginia coast. Karen is now about two hundred miles off the coast of Delaware, traveling due north/ northeast at seventeen miles per hour. The National Weather Service now predicts that Karen will make landfall in New Jersey or possibly Long Island, New York, within forty-eight hours."

Long Island! That was right next to Connecticut. Suddenly I felt worried. Was there a chance we would get hit by the hurricane? On the news I had seen people nailing boards over their windows and buying bottled water and canned foods. It had looked scary. I did not want to get hit by a hurricane, not even if it was named Karen.

I looked at Mommy, to see if she was worried too. But she just smiled at me and clicked off the television. "Well, that was interesting," she said. "Now get your things, Karen. It is time to go to school."

Mommy did not seem worried, so I felt better. At least for now.

In all the excitement over Hurricane Karen, I had almost forgotten that Friday was Fix-Up Day at school. Thank goodness I had remembered in time to dress in a T-shirt, overalls, and work boots. (That is my working-in-the-garden outfit.)

After Addie Sidney took attendance, my class went outside. We were all dressed for a day of working in the gardens. It was a beautiful September morning — clear and warm, with a hint of fall in the air. It was strange to think that a terrible storm might be heading in our direction. I kept glancing at the sky, but all I saw was blue sky and a few puffy, white clouds.

While Ms. Colman was explaining which shrubs would be planted where, I sat with Hannie and Nancy under the old oak. We pretended we were princess sisters who were under a spell and made to look like farmers.

Next to the maintenance room were many black plastic buckets with small shrubs in them. There were five different kinds of plants, of different sizes.

Next to the plants was a huge stack of

bags of mulch. There was also a small wagon filled with cotton work gloves, small hand trowels, a larger shovel, and some little garden rakes.

Ms. Colman looked at us Three Musketeers. "Girls, would you like to be one team?" she asked.

"Yes!" we cried.

Ms. Colman picked out six of the smaller shrubs and set them close to us. "Here are six little box hedges. These need to go in a straight line over here, by this walkway."

The walkway was about thirty feet from the old oak. Ms. Colman explained that each plant would need a hole about twice as wide and twice as deep as the plastic pot that held the shrub. Hannie, Nancy, and I nodded.

Then Ms. Colman stuck six short stakes in the ground, each a couple of feet apart, to show where we were to dig. She placed a shrub next to each stake.

"Two holes apiece should be plenty of digging," Ms. Colman said. "When the holes are done, I will come back and help you set your plants in the ground. Okay?"

"Okay," we answered.

Ms. Colman handed us each a spade, said, "Happy digging," and moved off with the wagon.

Now we pretended to be enchanted princess sisters who dug holes for a living. Digging is hard work! Luckily, even though we were pretty far from the oak, we were in its shade. Our old friend was keeping us cool.

When we were done digging and Ms. Colman returned, I asked her, "How old do you suppose that oak tree is, Ms. Colman?"

Ms. Colman looked up from where she was patting soil around the base of a newly planted box hedge.

"Oh, my, I could not say for sure," she said. "But judging from its size, I would guess that it is seventy or eighty years old. Possibly older."

"Older than eighty years?" I said. "Wow. That is ancient."

"It certainly is," Ms. Colman agreed.

As I put my little shrubs into their holes, I said to them, "You youngsters behave yourselves. You are in the shadow of a grand old tree."

Hannie and Nancy giggled.

Hurricane Preparations

On Saturday, Mommy, Seth, Andrew, and I watched the news three times. We wanted to know what Hurricane Karen was doing. By Sunday morning, it was starting to look as if Hurricane Karen would not hit New Jersey, but would make landfall at Long Island instead. Hurricanes like to keep people guessing! It seemed as if every time we watched the news, the hurricane had done something new that surprised people. (Sometimes I am like that myself.)

If Hurricane Karen went across Long Island, it would then pass over Long Island Sound. (Long Island Sound is a narrow sliver of the Atlantic Ocean.) Then it would hit land again — either in Rhode Island or Connecticut!

When the television news reporters said that people in Connecticut should start preparing to possibly get hit by Hurricane Karen, I felt a shiver go up my spine. This hurricane was practically the scariest thing I could imagine.

"How do we prepare ourselves?" I asked Mommy and Seth.

"Should we get our raincoats and boots ready?" asked Andrew.

"That would be a start," said Mommy. "But I am afraid we will have to do much more than that."

"If Stoneybrook takes a direct hit," said Seth, "we may lose our electricity for several days. The refrigerator will not run, and we will not be able to cook food. Also, floodwaters could possibly make our tap water undrinkable."

"Oh, no," I said. I had had no idea that a storm — even a hurricane — could do all that. I held Mommy's hand.

"We must remember that it may not hit us after all," Mommy said. "But in any case, it is good to be prepared. I am planning to go to the supermarket to buy canned food, bottled water, candles, and other things we may need. Would you like to come with me, Karen?"

"Definitely," I said.

"Andrew can come with me to the hardware store," said Seth. "I need to pick up batteries for flashlights, radios, and our portable television set, so we can watch the news even if the electricity goes out. And I will swing by the shop to pick up some plywood to nail over the picture window downstairs."

"Plywood over the windows?" I said. Just like the people we had seen on TV.

"It is just to be safe," said Mommy. "We want to protect the glass from the high winds."

I glanced at Andrew. He looked as frightened as I felt. Here it was again: I had to be a good big sister, no matter how scared I felt myself. "Oh, boy!" I made myself say. "This is going to be fun and exciting."

I glanced at Andrew again. He did not look like he thought the hurricane was going to be fun.

"Ready to go to the hardware store, sport?" Seth asked Andrew.

Andrew nodded seriously.

The supermarket was very crowded when we got there. It seemed as if everybody in Stoneybrook were there to buy canned goods, candles, and water. I saw Omar Harris and his dad, Addie Sidney and her mom, and one of the people who works in the school cafeteria.

Mommy and I took six gallon jugs of water off the shelf. There were only a few more left. The stockboy said there might be more the next morning, but not to count on it. I hoped Daddy and Elizabeth had already

bought their water. Mommy told me that when we got home I could call the big house to make sure they were prepared.

You know what? I decided I did not like hurricanes one tiny bit, even if they were named after me.

8

Hurricane Warning

On Monday morning at school, everyone was talking about Karen. Hurricane Karen, that is.

I had watched the news on TV in the morning before school. It had felt strange to watch TV while I was eating my Krispy Krunchies. The latest prediction was that the storm would strike the coast of Connecticut within twenty-four hours. We were officially on a hurricane watch. Even though the weatherwoman was not one hundred percent sure, it looked as if Hurricane Karen might be headed our way.

"My dad boarded up all our windows," said Ian Johnson.

"We have enough canned green beans to last until December," said Sara Ford. "I hate canned green beans."

"We might leave town if it looks like the hurricane is going to hit Stoneybrook," said Pamela Harding, my best enemy. "Mommy has relatives in Pennsylvania. She said if the hurricane comes here, we will just get in our car and go."

That figures, I said to myself. It is just like Pamela to get going when the going gets rough. (I will tell you a secret. Even though I said this to myself, a little tiny eensy-weensy part of me wished my family and I were going someplace else too.)

"My family is staying," I said firmly, trying to talk myself into being brave. "My stepfather, Seth, said he would help board up stores downtown. We are as prepared as we can be. We believe in sticking around

44

and helping others during tough times," I added pointedly.

Pamela sniffed and stuck her nose in the air.

When the bell rang, Ms. Colman asked me to take attendance. Usually I am gigundoly happy when it is my turn. But today my mind was on the hurricane.

During reading that morning, Ms. Colman tried to review our context clues. I love context clues, but no one could pay attention. Even Ms. Colman seemed a little distracted.

Finally she said, "Well, class, it seems that we are not likely to get much work done today. I am as anxious as you all are. So why don't we have individual reading time for half an — "

Just then the voice of Mrs. Titus, the principal, came over the loudspeaker. I jumped in my seat. Mrs. Titus hardly ever uses the loudspeaker.

"Attention, attention, please, all classes," came Mrs. Titus's voice. "An actual hurricane warning, not a watch, has just been issued for a wide area of Connecticut, including Stoneybrook and the surrounding towns."

I gasped and turned to look at Hannie and Nancy. Their eyes were big and round.

"Classes are being dismissed for the day, so that students and teachers can get home safely and prepare for the hurricane," said Mrs. Titus.

I put my hand over my mouth. Oh my goodness! Hurricane Karen was heading for Stoneybrook!

Hurricane Karen Strikes

It took a long time to contact everyone's parents. Thank goodness Mommy was at the crafts center. When the school secretary called her, she came right away. On our way home, we picked up Andrew from preschool. Merry Perkins went home early so she would not get caught in the storm. I told her to take care of herself.

Mommy, Andrew, and I ate lunch quietly. We all kept looking at the sky. It had been dark and cloudy all day, but by afternoon it began to rain. There was a strong breeze. Already I could see leaves and twigs flying through the air.

"Is this the hurricane already?" I asked Mommy.

"It is the hurricane's leading edge," Mommy explained. "The storm will get much stronger during the night."

I was so happy when Seth came home. I felt safer somehow, and I know Mommy did too. Mommy made an extra-special dinner that night to cheer us up, and guess what. For dessert, we tried to eat every bit of ice cream in our freezer!

"After all, if we lose power, the ice cream will go bad," said Mommy, scooping it out. "We cannot let food go to waste."

Andrew and I smiled at each other.

After dinner, Seth nailed large pieces of plywood over our picture window downstairs. Mommy, Andrew, and I went around our house putting long strips of masking tape over our other windows. It was to help keep them from breaking. And it would hold the glass together if the windows did break.

That night, I could not fall asleep. Neither could Andrew. We wound up in bed with Mommy and Seth. I know that was kind of babyish, but we could not help it. The storm was getting louder and louder. Rocky and Midgie were already hiding under the bed.

Mommy sang a song that went, "Que será, será. Whatever will be, will be."

I must have fallen asleep finally, because the next thing I knew I was in my own bed and a murky light was showing in my window. And goodness gracious, was the wind ever blowing! I pulled back my curtain. Rain splattered against the glass as if someone were shooting a hose at it.

I ran downstairs. Mommy was in the kitchen, drinking a cup of coffee.

"Is this the hurricane?" I yelled over the howling of the wind. I looked at the ceiling. The light was on. We had not lost power yet.

Mommy nodded. "This certainly is," she shouted back.

Just then Andrew padded into the room in his footy pajamas. There was a tremendous crack of thunder. Andrew burst into tears and ran into Mommy's arms.

"Okay," she said, patting his back and hugging him. "It is only a little thunder."

Suddenly I felt like I needed a hug too. I hurried to Mommy, and she held me tight.

Then I realized something. "Where is Seth?" I asked. "Is he still asleep?"

"He left a couple of hours ago, just before the storm got bad," Mommy said. "He was going downtown, to see if anybody needed help with last-minute storm-proofing."

"He is outside in a hurricane?" I asked, shocked.

"Seth will be fine," Mommy said. "You do not need to be worried about him."

But I was.

I had never seen rain come down so hard. There was no space at all between the raindrops. At times the wind blew so hard that the rain did not seem to be falling. It was just flying straight across the ground.

Other things were flying around too. Andrew and I saw leaves, sticks, branches, bits of trash, a garbage-can lid, a cardboard box, a plastic lawn chair, and the garbage can that went with the garbage-can lid all go skittering and bouncing down the street. Our gutters ran deep with rain, and the water was flowing fast, like a stream.

And the thunder and lightning! At first Andrew was terrified of the thunder (I did not like it much myself), but after a few hours he got used to it. There was just so much of it that it was impossible to be terrified by every single crash. But we wrapped my blanket around our shoulders to feel cozy and snug, and held hands.

Around ten o'clock we lost electricity in the house. My room suddenly went dark, almost as dark as night.

"Are you guys okay up there?" called Mommy from downstairs.

Andrew and I felt not so okay, but he nodded at me. "Yes," I called back. "We are fine."

"All right," said Mommy. "Please be careful on the stairs if you come down. I will turn on the battery-operated radio to listen for information about the storm."

Andrew and I sat silently and watched the amazing storm outside. After awhile, Mommy came upstairs and sat with us. She put her arms around us.

"The radio says the eye of the storm is headed this way," she said. "That means this hurricane will feel worse for us before it feels better." She smiled and hugged us. "I am so thankful to have you both with me here, safe."

I had an idea. Seth was out somewhere, where we could not call him. But what about my big-house family? I could call them. Were they all right? Were they frightened? Did they have candles and batteries?

"Mommy, may I call the big house?" I asked.

"Yes, that is a good idea," said Mommy.

I jumped up and ran to the phone. But when I picked up the receiver, there was no dial tone. Our phones had gone dead.

The Eye of the Storm

By three in the afternoon, I could not believe that a storm could be so fierce for so long. I was sure our street must be flooded with water. Would our house wash away? I pictured the little house swirling like a leaf down a river of water, while Mommy and Andrew and I yelled for help from the windows. I shivered.

And still the thunder boomed and the rain came down and the wind howled.

All of a sudden, I heard a roaring in my ears. A new kind of roaring. My ears felt like they were ringing. "What is that?" I wondered out loud. Then I realized: It was silence. My ears were so used to hearing the storm that now they were surprised to be hearing nothing.

There was no rain pelting our windows. There was no wind howling like an angry monster. There were no leaves and twigs clicking against the sides of our house. Listening hard, I could make out only the faint echo of thunder a long way off.

"Mommy, Mommy!" I called, dashing downstairs. Andrew pattered after me. "The hurricane is over!"

"I am afraid not," Mommy said. "This is only the eye of the storm. Right in the middle of a hurricane is a small area of quiet. That is what you hear now. We are only halfway through Hurricane Karen."

"Halfway?" Andrew wailed. He collapsed on the couch and buried his face in a cushion.

I felt like doing the same thing. But I stopped myself because I was trying to be a good, brave big sister. We were only halfway through the hurricane? I could not believe it.

"Where is Seth?" Andrew howled. "I want Seth!" He burst into tears again.

Good, brave big sister or not, I could not help myself. I burst into tears along with him. "I want Seth too! And I want to talk to Daddy and Nannie and Kristy!"

For the second time that day, Mommy held us and comforted us. The three of us curled up on the couch together. (Rocky and Midgie were still upstairs under Mommy's bed.)

"Please do not worry about Seth," said Mommy.

"But you do not know where he is," I pointed out.

"True. But I am absolutely certain that he is safe. Seth is a very careful and thoughtful person. He would not take unnecessary risks. And he had plenty of time to get into a shelter before the storm became bad. Now come on," she said, when we had finished snuffling. "Would you like to go out on the porch and see what Hurricane Karen has done to our front yard?"

We stepped onto the porch and looked at the street. Actually, we could not see the street. It was covered with water. The water came halfway up our lawn. It looked as if we lived on a river. I saw a tire float by, and a long plank of wood. Shreds of paper, old soda cans, and other trash floated by too.

"Look, there is a lawn chair," said Andrew, pointing.

"There is a bird feeder," I said.

Everywhere we looked, sticks and bits of leaves and grass floated by us. What a mess.

"Wow," I whispered. "How deep is the water?"

"Look at the stop sign at the corner," Mommy said. "The water is about a foot up the sign's pole. I would guess that means that the water is about a foot and a half deep in the street."

"Gosh," said Andrew.

"Seth will not be able to drive his truck through this water, will he?" I asked.

"No," said Mommy. "He will have to wait for the water to go down before he can come home."

"How long will that take?" asked Andrew.

"I am not sure."

Mommy was trying to sound calm, but I could tell she was worried too.

We stared in wonder at the water for awhile. My nice familiar old neighborhood looked weird under a foot and a half of water.

Finally Mommy said, "I am going inside to get the portable TV. I want to see if there is any news on the hurricane. I will be right back." Since there was no electricity inside, there was more light to see by outside. Now I knew how the pioneers felt.

In a minute Mommy returned, and she clicked on the TV. (It is a tiny battery-operated TV. The screen is not much bigger than a saltine cracker.)

"This is Ken Handy, live from downtown Stoneybrook," said a teeny-tiny reporter on the teeny-tiny TV. "I have received reports of flooding and minor wind damage to buildings. With me is Seth Engle, a volunteer worker who was helping prepare for the hurricane when the storm hit. Mr. Engle, what have you seen?"

I squealed, and Mommy, Andrew, and I all peered closely at the screen. I gripped Mommy's hand, and she squeezed back. I do not think she knew how hard she was squeezing.

The screen showed a teeny-tiny Seth. He looked fine.

"Well, Ken, I have been sitting out the storm in the fire station, and we have had no reports of — " Seth began.

But I never heard the rest of what he said. Mommy and Andrew and I were jumping up and down and yelling hooray. We were so happy to see that Seth was safe.

We quieted down just in time to hear Seth say, "And I would like to say hello to my wife, Lisa, and to Karen and Andrew. I am safe, you guys, and I will be home when the storm is over."

"Yea!" the three of us shouted.

"Thank you, Mr. Engle," said the reporter. He turned to the camera. "This is Ken Handy, live from Stoneybrook. Ted?"

Then the anchorman took over.

Mommy, Andrew, and I hugged all over again. Seth was okay!

Shadows on the Wall

The eye of the hurricane lasted two hours. It was eerily calm all that time. Right before dinner the wind and rain started up again as suddenly as they had stopped earlier. Even though there was more than an hour of daylight left, when the clouds moved in, it became as dark as night. And without electricity, we had to burn candles to see inside the house.

"I think this is romantic," said Mommy cheerfully as we ate our dinner by candle-light.

"It is cozy," I agreed, being the brave big sister again. "I can hardly hear the wind outside."

"How can you not hear the wind?" Andrew sounded grumpy. "It sounds like the house is going to blow down."

I took a bite of my sandwich. Mommy put some more chips on my plate. "Pretend it is the Big Bad Wolf," I said. "And we are the Three Little Pigs."

"And we are safe and snug inside our little brick house," added Mommy.

Andrew grinned. He yelled, "You cannot come in! Not by the hair on our chinny-chin-chins!" He looked better. Mommy and I smiled at each other.

After dinner Mommy set up the flashlight on the living room table and shone it toward the wall. Then she used her hands to make shadow animals. She made a crocodile, a rabbit, a dog, a bird, a spider, and a camel (her head made the hump).

Andrew and I tried it too. We could make most of them, though my camel looked more like a fat giraffe. (Andrew's looked the same as his rabbit.)

Then we read by candlelight for awhile. I felt like a pioneer girl again. The house was becoming very stuffy. We could not open the windows because of all the wind and rain. But the storm seemed to be dying down a bit.

That night Andrew and I did not take baths. Our bathtub was full of water that we would need to use for washing dishes, and ourselves, if our running water got turned off. (It had not been, so far.) At bedtime Mommy tucked me in and kissed me good night. She put a flashlight next to my bed, in case I had to get up during the night to go to the bathroom.

"You were very brave today, Karen," said Mommy. "And you were a big help with Andrew."

"Was I?" I asked. I had really tried.

Mommy nodded. "I am proud of you and Andrew, and of Seth," she said.

"I am proud of Seth too," I said. "I am glad he is downtown helping other people, even if we do miss him. At least we know that he is okay."

"That is right," Mommy said. "Seth will come home tomorrow, and the hurricane will be over. Now, good night, sweetheart."

"Good night, Mommy."

After Mommy left, I took the flashlight and went to my window that looks out onto Nancy's house next door. I aimed the flashlight toward her bedroom window and clicked it on. The beam of the flashlight showed the rain still coming down hard, even though the wind was not so fierce. I clicked the flashlight off. On again. Off. On. Off. This was the secret signal that we had agreed on. During the eye of the storm, I had called to Nancy from my porch. But she had not come out. I guessed her mommy and daddy wanted her to stay inside.

I waited for a minute. Suddenly I saw a bright circle of light in Nancy's window. She had turned on her flashlight. Then it went dark. It came on again. Then off. She was okay!

I giggled, then flashed her back once. She flashed me back.

We were saying hello.

I wished that we had made up a code. We could have sent messages back and forth, like "How are you?" and "Fine. How are you?" and "What did you have for dinner?"

But we could not say any of those things with no code. And suddenly I was feeling very tired. I had had a long and exciting day.

I clicked my flashlight on and off twice quickly. I hoped Nancy would understand that I was saying good night.

She flashed twice quickly back at me.

She had understood.

I made up my mind to have a code all ready for our next hurricane.

Captain Kristy

When I woke up the next morning, the first thing I noticed was — no howling wind! I looked out my window. There was a light drizzle. And there were branches and twigs and leaves all over the yard. And the street was still covered with water.

But no wind, no heavy rain, no thunder and lightning. Hurricane Karen was over.

For breakfast we ate untoasted bagels with lukewarm jam and lukewarm juice.

"I am afraid we still have no electricity and no phone," said Mommy. "We have about six inches of water in our cellar. And there is no school today."

"Cool!" said Andrew. "Can we put on our boots and explore the cellar?"

"Oh, no," said Mommy. "It is not safe. When Seth comes home, he will set up a small pump, to pump out the water."

"I was hoping Seth would be home when I got up," I said.

"I am sure he is still downtown, helping people clean up," said Mommy. "And with all the water in the streets, he cannot drive home yet anyway. He will have to wait until the water goes down."

"When will that be?" asked Andrew.

Mommy shrugged. "I am not sure. Stoneybrook has never been flooded before."

After breakfast Mommy said it was okay for me to go across the yard to Nancy's house. I was not to go into the street, however, where the water was.

I pulled on my boots and rain slicker, put on my rain hat (it is yellow with pink daisies), and went outside. The ground was squishy underneath my boots, and I had to step carefully to keep from tripping over fallen branches.

I knocked on Nancy's back door.

"Karen!" Nancy said, flinging open the door. "Let me get my boots and I will come outside with you." Pulling on her boots, she called out, "Did you think your hurricane was exciting? I thought it was scary."

As soon as she was out the door, we started asking questions and answering them at the same time: "Are your phone and lights working?" "Neither are ours!" "Do you have water in your cellar?" "So do we!" "The wind was so, so loud!" "It sure was!"

I was gigundoly glad to see Nancy, and she was glad to see me too. We talked and talked and talked. We agreed that we would for sure have a flashlight code worked out in time for the next hurricane. (In fact, we started on it right then and there. We agreed on two quick flashes for "How are you?" and three quick flashes for "I am fine.")

It had stopped drizzling. We had wandered around to the front of Nancy's house. The street was still full of water. But I thought maybe it had gone down a little. I saw a large branch float by, and it looked like an alligator. Nancy and I pretended we were princesses stranded on a desert island, surrounded by alligators.

I shaded my eyes and peered into the distance. "Oh, no, Princess Nancy! I fear I do not see help!" (Princesses talk that way.) Then I squinted and pushed my glasses up on my nose. It looked like . . . was that a boat coming up our street?

"What is that?" asked Nancy, pointing.

"It is a rowboat!" I said excitedly. "Someone is rowing up our street!"

"It looks like Mr. Engle!" said Nancy, amazed.

"And . . . Kristy!" I shouted.

It was true. My stepsister, Kristy, was rowing Seth up our street in a small rowboat.

"Ahoy there, matey," Kristy called, waving a paddle. The rowboat glided closer to our front lawn. It bumped a bit against our curb. It was the weirdest sight I had ever seen. "Captain Kristy requests permission to tie up at your dock. I have a passenger who misses his family very much."

I looked at Nancy. She looked at me. Our mouths were hanging open.

"Permission granted, Captain Kristy!" I called to her.

After the Storm

"Hi, Karen! Hi, Nancy!" said Seth as he and Kristy came ashore onto our porch. "Boy, am I glad to be home!"

I gave Seth a big hug. "I am glad you are home too!"

Just then Mommy and Andrew came out of our house and saw Seth. They ran to him and threw their arms around him also. While we were standing there hugging, Nancy's mommy called her back into her house.

" 'Bye, Karen," said Nancy.

" 'Bye, Nancy. I will talk to you later."

My family finished up its hug, and Mommy said to Seth, "I see Kristy brought you home."

"That is right," said Seth. "I spent all yesterday helping people downtown battle the wind and rain. The volunteer firemen gave me a bunk at the station for the night, though I got only a few hours' sleep. I was helping with the cleanup this morning when I suddenly realized how exhausted I was. I decided to head for home even if I had to walk the whole way. I was wading up Hyslip Street when Kristy came along and offered me a lift."

"Where is your truck?" I asked.

"I left it on the second floor of the parking garage downtown," said Seth. "I am not sure when I will be able to drive it home. Still, at least it is safe. A lot of cars that were parked in the street have been flooded."

Seth sighed. I could see that he was worn out. "Well, I would like a hot shower and a warm bed now," he said. He turned to

Kristy. "Thank you very much for the ride, Captain." He saluted her.

"My pleasure," said Kristy. "And now I think I will go back downtown."

Suddenly I was dying to see what Hurricane Karen had done to Stoneybrook. "Mommy, may I go with Kristy?" I asked.

"Do you think it is safe?" Mommy asked Seth.

"Yes," said Seth. "The water is very calm, and it comes up only to her knees."

"All right, Karen, but be careful," said Mommy.

I climbed into the rowboat, and Kristy shoved off from shore.

"Good-bye!" I called.

"Bon voyage!" called Mommy.

A Cruise Downtown

"How is everyone at the big house?" I asked Kristy as she paddled down Forest Drive.

"Fine," Kristy said. "A big branch split off from the sycamore in the backyard, but that was the worst of the damage. I saw Hannie, and she told me to tell you she was fine too."

"Whew!" I said. I wiped imaginary sweat off my brow. "That is a relief. I was really worried about you guys."

"We were worried about you too," said Kristy, patting my knee. I love my stepsister.

Pretty soon we left Forest Drive and turned onto one street after another until at last we were on Essex Road, heading downtown. We passed by Thelma's Café. Big sheets of plywood had been nailed over the windows, as if it had gone out of business. The plywood had done its job, though. Thelma's did not look damaged by the hurricane.

"Oh, no, Karen," said Kristy suddenly. "Look." She pointed with her paddle at a store coming up on the left. It was Greetings, a card shop. From where we were, it looked as if half the roof of the shop had been blown off. Jutting out of the top of the store was a tangle of twisted metal with big black shingles hanging off of it. A couple of firefighters in hip boots waded around in front of Greetings, talking into walkie-talkies.

"Can we do anything to help?" Kristy called to the firefighters.

"I am afraid not," one called back. "All we can do now is clean up."

Kristy steered the boat back to Rosedale Road and over to Spring Street, then up Main Street through downtown Stoneybrook. We saw many, many broken windows, lots of signs ripped off of buildings, and three or four more buildings with missing roofs. I thought how lucky our little house had been, and how cozy and safe Mommy and Andrew and I had been in the storm.

All the cars that were parked downtown were sitting in water that came up to the tops of their tires. I wondered if they were ruined.

According to another fireman, almost every business in town had water on the first floor.

Kristy and I hardly said a word as we paddled around, looking over the damage. It seemed as if it would be months, years even, before things would look normal again. I could not believe this could have happened to Stoneybrook. But it had.

I felt like crying.

"I feel like crying," I said to Kristy as we turned up Reilly Lane.

"Me too, Karen," said Kristy. "Me too."

After a few minutes, Kristy said, "I have seen enough. I will take you home now, okay?"

I nodded. I was too upset to say anything.

Kristy paddled me home without saying another word either.

A Terrible Tragedy

By Wednesday night most of the water had drained out of the street in front of the little house. Our street looked messy and yucky, though. I did not know how it would ever get clean again.

All day Wednesday, we had listened to either the radio or the little TV. Three towns nearby had also suffered a lot of damage. On Thursday morning, the TV announcer said that most of the water from downtown was gone. But even after most of the water was gone, our town smelled swampy and stale and yucky.

The little house did not get its electricity back until Thursday night. (We knew it was back because suddenly half the lights in the house came on.) Parts of Stoneybrook did not have electricity until Friday afternoon.

School was canceled for the rest of that week. I love school, but it is nice to have an unexpected vacation. Actually, it was not much of a vacation. Mommy, Seth, Andrew, and I tried to clean up our yard. We raked up piles of stuff, put it in garbage bags, and swept our walk. Seth shoveled mud and silt out of our street gutter, so the drain would not be blocked if it rained again. And we all helped clean up the basement.

I was glad when school opened again on Monday.

That morning Nancy and I met Hannie on the playground in front of the school, as usual. There were still leaves and sticks and branches left over from the storm scattered all over the ground. In the middle of the playground there was still a gigundo puddle. (My pretend husband, Ricky Torres, named it Lake Stoneybrook.) There was more damage at Stoneybrook Academy than practically anywhere else in town. A bunch of windows had been blown out (none in Ms. Colman's room, thank goodness!). The flagpole in front of the school had been bent in half like a straw. Shrubs and bushes had been torn out of the ground.

"All the work we did on Fix-Up Day was ruined by Hurricane Karen," said Hannie, frowning.

"It is so sad," said Nancy. "I like our school to look nice. The playground looks like a disaster area."

"I heard Bobby Gianelli say we would be having recess inside until the puddle dries up," I said.

The three of us groaned. Outdoor recess is much more fun than indoor recess.

"Come on. Let's go around to the back of

82

the school to see if the shrubs we planted are all right," I suggested.

"Okay," said Hannie and Nancy.

It was then that we discovered a terrible tragedy.

Our shrubs had been ripped up by the hurricane. But that was not the terrible tragedy. (We had almost expected that.) The terrible tragedy was that the old oak, our favorite tree in the whole entire world, was lying on its side, ripped up by the roots.

We stood in shock, not saying anything for a long, long time. The proud old oak looked so sad, with its branches and trunk in the mud, and half its roots flung up into the air. There was a huge hole in the ground, filled with muddy brown water, where the roots had been.

Someone had discovered the fallen oak before we had — bright orange tape had been staked all the way around it, to keep people away.

"Oh, Nancy! Hannie!" I said at last. "This is just awful!"

How to Say Good-bye?

Before class started, everyone was talking about Hurricane Karen.

"We lost some shingles off our roof," said Ian.

"That is nothing," said Sara. "My dog Frederick's doghouse blew over on its side — and then it floated away! We did not find it until Saturday, in our neighbor's yard, three houses down."

"My uncle Vic bought a brand-new sports car two weeks ago," said Natalie Springer as she pulled up her socks. "He left it parked in the street, and it was flooded up to the dashboard. He was practically crying. He said it was totally ruined."

Almost everyone had an exciting story to tell — except Pamela Harding. She and her parents had gone to Pennsylvania to avoid the storm. She tried to show everyone the new pair of shoes she had bought, but the kids were more interested in the hurricane. Ha! Pamela had missed all the excitement.

When the bell rang, Ms. Colman called our class to order. "Well, we have had a thrilling week. It is too bad, though, that our good work on Fix-Up Day was undone by Hurricane Karen. Almost all our plantings were torn up by the wind or washed away by the rain."

I raised my hand. "Ms. Colman? What about the old oak? Can it . . . ?" Suddenly a lump formed in my throat. I could hardly even ask the question. "Can it be saved?"

Ms. Colman looked very serious and very sad. "I am afraid not, Karen. Once a big tree like that has been knocked over, there is nothing anyone can do for it. Workers will come to cut it up and haul it away."

I could feel tears welling up in my eyes. It was so, so sad to think that our old oak would soon be gone forever. Sawed up into firewood.

"What about a crane?" asked Ricky Torres. "A crane could lift it up and stick it back in its hole."

Yes! That was a great idea. I turned to Ricky and gave him a smile.

Ms. Colman just shook her head. "That would not work, Ricky. The tree's roots are damaged. It would not survive, even if it were upright again."

The class was silent for awhile. I think we all felt sad about the loss of the wonderful old tree. I wished I could think of a way to say good-bye to it. But how? Have a funeral for it and put up a gravestone where it used to stand? That did not seem right. But the idea of a marker of some kind was not bad. When my fish Crystal Light the First died, we buried her in the backyard and made a little marker. Our old oak friend should have a much bigger marker than a small fish had.

For Fix-Up Day I had wanted my class to do something more special than just plant shrubs. Now maybe we could do something more. We could put up a sign in honor of the old oak, or something like that. But a sign was still not quite right. . . .

Oh. My. Gosh. Suddenly I had the most brilliant idea ever. It was the perfect way to do something special in honor of our tree, *and* something special for the school! I wiggled in my seat with excitement. I started to raise my hand, to tell Ms. Colman my idea, but then I stopped. There was someone I needed to talk to first.

I needed to talk to Seth.

Karen's Idea

When I get an idea, it is very hard for me not to tell everyone about it right away. But this was such a great idea, and such an important one, that I kept it inside me like a treasure all day at school, all afternoon, and even all through dinner.

After dinner, I finally let it out.

"Mommy, Seth, you know the big old oak tree at school?" I began.

"Yes," said Mommy. "When I drove by there this morning, I saw that it had been knocked over by the storm. How terrible!"

"Well, I have been thinking," I said. And I told them how much the oak meant to my friends and me, and how it was going to be cut up and hauled away. And I told them how I wanted to honor the oak somehow.

"This is my idea," I said. "Instead of letting the tree be turned into firewood, maybe someone" — I cast a glance at Seth — "could build something out of the wood? Like a bench, a beautiful bench for people to sit on and enjoy the outdoors."

I looked around the table. Andrew was humming to himself and carving something out of his mashed potatoes. (I did not think he had been paying attention.) Mommy was looking at Seth. Seth was looking at me.

I waited. No one said anything for a moment.

"That is a wonderful idea, Karen," said Seth. "And I will be happy to do it. I believe I can make a very special bench out of the oak."

"Hooray!" I shouted.

Andrew jumped in his chair. "What? What?" he asked.

"Seth is going to make a bench out of the tree that was knocked down at school," I explained.

"Oh." Andrew went back to sculpting his potatoes.

"Before you get too excited, Karen," said Seth, "we should call Ms. Colman. Perhaps the school already has plans for the wood, or for the place where the tree used to stand."

I nodded. "Okay. Can we check with Ms. Colman now?"

Seth went right to the phone and called Ms. Colman. He must have thought this was very important, since my parents hardly ever call Ms. Colman at home.

Seth told Ms. Colman about my idea for the bench. Then he said that if the school were willing to give the wood to him, he would make a bench out of it and donate it back to the school.

There was a pause while Seth listened to

Ms. Colman talk. I crossed my fingers for luck. I crossed my toes for more luck. I thought about all the hairs on my head that were crossed, and hoped they were lucky too.

Seth hung up the phone and smiled at me. "Ms. Colman thinks it is a terrific idea," he said. "And as far as she knows, the school has no plans for either the wood or the spot where the tree is. She needs to talk to the principal. But it looks as if I am going to be making a bench."

For the second time that evening, I shouted, "Hooray!"

And for the second time, Andrew jumped and said, "What? What?"

I laughed. "Never mind, Andrew. Go back to your potatoes."

Good as New (Almost)

One afternoon two weeks later, I decided to walk to Seth's shop after school. (His shop is only four blocks away from the little house.) Merry gave me permission to go as long as I 1) looked both ways before I crossed every street, 2) stayed on the sidewalk, 3) went straight to Seth's shop with no detours, and 4) came straight home afterward with no detours. I promised I would follow all these rules.

In case you are wondering, I will tell you that Mrs. Titus had loved my idea about how to remember the special oak tree. Now the bench was finished, and it was time for me to see it. Since it was all my idea, I got to be the very first person to see the bench (except for Seth). I was so tingly with excitement that I bounced instead of walked.

It was a beautiful day. It was bright and sunny, and the air smelled especially nice. I decided that fall is the perfect time of year.

As I bounced along, I looked at everything in my neighborhood as if I had never seen it before. It looked much better than it had just a short while ago. The street was not filled with muddy water and leaves. No big branches were lying on anyone's lawn, and no trash was anywhere. Windows were not boarded up with plywood, and there were no broken windows either. Yards had been raked, sidewalks swept, trees and bushes trimmed. Everything looked fresh and clean and whole.

Even Greetings, the card shop that had lost part of its roof, was open for business.

"Hi, Karen!" a voice called.

I looked up to see Kristy waving to me from her bicycle.

"Hi, Kristy!" I waved back. "What are you doing around here?" I asked. (The big house is practically all the way across town.)

Kristy came to a stop. She pointed to the camera hanging around her neck. "I am writing an article for my school newspaper," she said. "About how our town has recovered from the hurricane." She looked around. "Pretty different from the day we rowed through town, huh?"

"That is exactly what I was thinking," I said. "Now everything seems as good as new."

"Well, almost as good as new," said Kristy. "I guess people here have a lot of strength and pride."

I nodded, feeling glad that I was a Stoneybrookian.

"Hurricane Karen seems far, far away now," said Kristy.

"It does," I agreed. "And you know what? It was fun to have a hurricane named after me, but next time I would like something nicer to be called Karen. Something small and quiet. Like a rose, maybe."

"The Karen Rose?" said Kristy thoughtfully. "That has a certain ring to it."

"It is better than Hurricane Karen, anyway," I said, laughing.

"Much better." Kristy gave me a hug, then hopped back on her bike and started pedaling away. "See you next week at the big house, Karen," she called.

" 'Bye, Kristy!"

The Beautiful Bench

A few minutes later I walked through the door of Seth's workshop. I sniffed deeply. I love the tangy, sawdusty smell there. It smells like fresh-cut wood, paint, and wax.

"Hey, Karen," said Seth, smiling up at me. "Come to see the finished product? Or almost finished, anyway. I am just putting a sealer on it."

Seth was brushing a shiny, clear liquid onto a long bench. I stepped closer and gazed at what my favorite oak tree had become. The bench was longer than I am tall. I could lie flat on it with plenty of room. (I mean, not then, because it was wet and sticky. But when it was dry, I could.) The seat was wide enough for grown-ups, but looked comfortable for children too. The arms and legs were made out of polished branches that had been left to look branch-like. But the back was the most special part. Seth had carved the top of the back with leaves, acorns, birds, and even two small squirrels, one at each end. After all, besides making shade for children, the oak had been a home to many creatures.

I did not know what to say. It was the most special, beautiful bench I had ever seen in my life. Seth is a very talented furniture-maker, but this bench looked as if it had been made by woodland fairies. Big ones.

"What do you think?" asked Seth.

"It is the most gigundoly beautiful bench in the world," I said solemnly. All of a sudden I felt as if I might cry. Seth had taken my idea, and the old oak tree, and joined them together into a wonderful new thing.

"You made my oak tree into something wonderful." My voice cracked a little. "If I cannot have the tree itself, this bench is good enough."

"Thank you, honey," said Seth.

"Why are you putting sealer on it?" I asked when I could talk again. "When it was a tree, no one put sealer on it."

"The tree had bark to protect it. Most of the bark is gone now," explained Seth. He took something small and shiny from a paper bag. "Look, I had a brass plate made. I am going to screw it onto the back of the bench, once the sealer is dry."

He handed me the plate. It said:

This bench was made of wood from an oak tree that grew for many, many years on this spot.

Presented to Stoneybrook Academy by Ms. Colman's second-grade class.

"Oh, Seth, that is perfect! Just perfect!" I said. I gave my stepfather a big, big hug.

The Unveiling

On Friday afternoon everyone in my school gathered in the yard. The yard still looked strange to me without the oak tree standing there. It was sunny, but kind of open and empty. Not as friendly. The huge hole where the tree's roots had been was now filled in with dirt and smoothed over. On the spot was a lumpy shape covered with a white sheet.

Mrs. Titus and Ms. Colman stood on either side of the lumpy shape. Seth and Mommy were with them.

I stood nearby with the other two Muske-teers. We waved to Seth and Mommy. (I had not told Hannie and Nancy what the bench looked like. I wanted them to be surprised. I hoped they would like it as much as I did.)

Mrs. Titus began to speak.

"For many years, students at Stoney-brook Academy gathered underneath a grand oak tree that grew on this spot," she said. "Friendships were made and strength-ened beneath its branches. Games were played around it. Lunches were eaten in its shade, when it was warm. In winter, its broad trunk provided protection from snowballs. Birds made nests in its branches, and squirrels gathered its acorns. In many different ways, that tree nurtured all of us who had the good fortune to be near it.

"Three weeks ago, tragedy struck our tree. The strong winds of Hurricane Karen knocked it over and pulled its roots from the ground. Many of us thought the tree's long and useful life had sadly come to an end.

"Then one of our students, who had a special love for the tree, came up with an idea to keep the spirit and memory of the tree alive. Thanks to the good thinking and kind heart of second-grader Karen Brewer" — she met my eye and smiled — "and the good work and imagination of her stepfather, Seth Engle, we will have a permanent and useful reminder of our old friend the oak."

I gripped Hannie's and Nancy's hands as Mrs. Titus pulled off the white sheet, revealing Seth's bench underneath. The crowd clapped and cheered. Hannie and Nancy both looked impressed and happy. I was so proud of Seth.

When everyone had quieted down, Mrs. Titus read the brass plate on the back of the bench. Everyone — especially the kids in Ms. Colman's class — cheered again. Ms. Colman smiled at me. I beamed. Then Ms. Colman said, "I would like to invite Karen Brewer to have the honor of being the first to sit on our new bench."

I took a deep breath. "I would be honored," I said in my most important-sounding voice.

Holding on to the other two Musketeers' hands, I stepped forward. "I want you two to come with me," I said to Hannie and Nancy. "We can have the honor together."

So the three of us sat down together, at the same time, on the bench. There was plenty of space for the three of us. In fact, two more kids could have fit on it. And the bench was very comfortable. We smiled big, and Mommy took our picture. A reporter for the *Stoneybrook News* also took a picture of us sitting on the bench, with Seth, Ms. Colman, and Mrs. Titus standing behind it. (I love having my picture taken.)

When the picture-taking was over, Ms. Colman said, "I have one more surprise. In the early spring, when planting time comes, we will plant an oak sapling behind the bench. In future years, the new tree will grow and cast its shadow, just as the old tree used to do."

"Yea!" Everyone cheered again. A brand-new tree! I would be able to watch it grow and grow. Years from now, when I was a grown-up, I could walk by Stoneybrook Academy and see the new oak. Children would be sitting on Seth's bench, giggling and whispering secrets. The new tree, grown big, would shade them with its leafy branches. I would stop and look at it, and remember the year that Hurricane Karen came to Stoneybrook.

L. GODWIN

About the Author

ANN M. MARTIN lives in New York City and loves animals, especially cats. She has two cats of her own, Gussie and Woody.

Other books by Ann M. Martin that you might enjoy are *Stage Fright*; *Me and Katie (the Pest)*; and the books in *The Baby-sitters Club* series.

Ann likes ice cream and *I Love Lucy*. And she has her own little sister, whose name is Jane.

Little Sister

Don't miss #114

KAREN'S CHICKEN POX

When I woke up on Wednesday, I felt worse than the day before. My little cold must have turned into a big one. That is what I thought. Then I looked in the mirror.

"Moosie, help!" I said to my stuffed cat. "I have spots!"

I jumped back into bed and pulled the covers over my head. I had to think of a plan. Maybe I could cover the spots with makeup. Elizabeth kept some in the bathroom. All I had to do was get in there without being seen.

I went to my door and peeked out. The coast was clear. I started to tiptoe to the bathroom. Just then Andrew stepped out of his room.

"Hi, Karen!" he said. "Ooh, you have spots!"